Eliza's Secret

by Mark Dubowski
illustrated by Mel Grant

POCKET
BOOKS

Pocket Books/Nickelodeon

New York   London   Toronto   Sydney   Singapore

POCKET
BOOKS

First published in Great Britain in 2003 by Pocket Books.
An imprint of Simon & Schuster UK Ltd
Africa House, 64-78 Kingsway, London WC2B 6AH

Originally published in 2002 by Simon Spotlight, an imprint of Simon & Schuster
Children's Publishing Division, New York.

A CIP catalogue record for this book is available from the British Library

ISBN 07434 61479

Printed and bound by Scotprint, Haddington

1 3 5 7 9 10 8 6 4 2

"There they are!" Eliza said. Eliza, Darwin and Donnie had been searching for Tally, a cheetah cub who had been snatched by poachers. Now, though, they were lost in the African rain forest and wanted to find their family.

"Mum, Dad!" Eliza called. But the people they saw were not her parents. They were Bree and Sloan Blackburn, wilderness researchers Eliza had met earlier that day.

"Sit down," said Bree, making room for Eliza by the fire. "You look exhausted."

"Thanks," Eliza said. "I'm looking for a cheetah cub who was taken by poachers."

"How awful!" Sloan said.

"I also heard poachers set up an electric fence in Tembo Valley to kill elephants for their tusks! I need to find my parents and tell them," Eliza said.

"How do you know that?" said Sloan.

A gorilla had told her – but Eliza couldn't tell that to Sloan. Shaman Mnyambo, who had given her the power to talk to animals, said she must keep it a secret.

"Don't worry, Eliza," Bree said. "We'll help you in the morning. You can all stay the night."

The next morning Donnie climbed into the Blackburn's van. "Don't go in there, Donnie!" Eliza said, running after him.

Just then Eliza heard a call for help. She opened a cupboard – and there was Tally, the missing cheetah cub! "Eliza, I knew you'd save me!" he cried.

"Sloan and Bree must be the poachers!" Eliza said.

Suddenly Sloan opened the door. "How do you know so much, you little troublemaker?" he asked, glaring at her.

"It was you! You built the electric fence!" Eliza yelled.

Sloan reached out to grab Eliza, but stopped when he heard the sound of an engine. Someone was coming!

It was Debbie in the Congo-Com! "Eliza, I've been looking all over for you!" she said.

But Sloan grabbed Debbie and brought her over to a cliff. "Tell me where you get your information, or she goes over!" he said to Eliza.

"Hey, what is your problem?" Debbie exclaimed. "Eliza, help!"

Eliza had promised she would never tell her secret. If she did, she knew she would lose her powers forever. Sloan moved Debbie closer to the edge of the cliff. Eliza had no choice!

She closed her eyes, took a deep breath and blurted out, "I know these things because I can talk to animals!"

At that moment lightning flashed and thunder boomed.

The wind howled and twisted around Eliza. Sloan and Bree made a run for their helicopter.

"Run, Debbie!" Eliza yelled. "We'll find the river. That will lead us to the valley!"

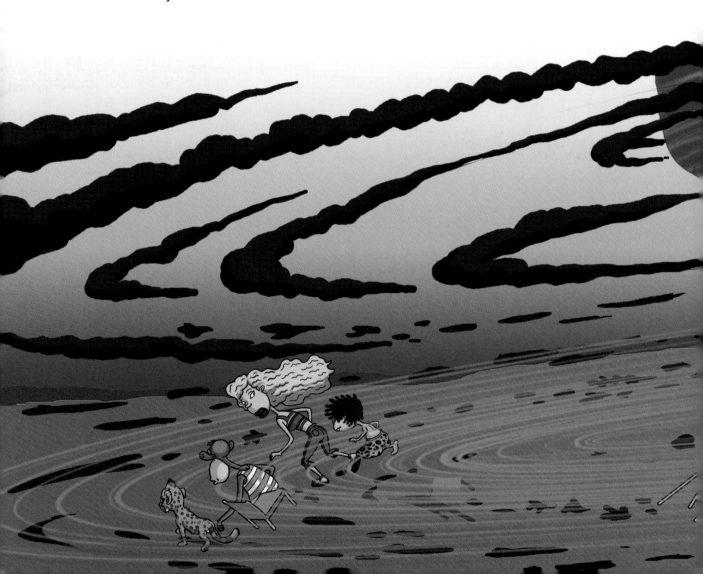

Darwin chittered something, but Eliza couldn't understand him. "It's true," she said to herself. "My powers are really gone!"

As they floated down the river on a log they found, Eliza told Debbie everything.

"You expect me to believe you freed a warthog, but he was really a magic man who made it so you could talk to animals, but you had to keep it a secret or else there'd be some tornado-thing and you would lose your powers?" Debbie said.

"Yeah," Eliza said. "And I broke the rule. I can't even understand Darwin any more."

"You did that," Debbie said, "for me?"

Before Eliza could answer, their log plowed into gravel on the shoreline. They stood on the shore and looked over the hill. Below them was a beautiful valley!

"This must be Tembo Valley," Eliza said. Then she heard a helicopter.

"Oh, no!" she exclaimed. "It's Sloan and Bree. The elephants are all going to die and I can't even warn them! I'm just an ordinary girl now."

Debbie shook her head. "Trust me, you were never ordinary," she told her sister. "You were born for this kind of thing!"

Eliza knew she had to do something. She ran down the side of the mountain and up to the herd of elephants. "Turn around!" she cried. "You'll all be killed!"

But they couldn't understand her. She saw an older female elephant leading the pack so Eliza climbed up on a rock and hopped onto the elephant's back!

"Please, you have to turn around!" Eliza begged. But the elephant kept walking.

"This way," Eliza said, pulling her trunk gently where she wanted her to go. She'd seen elephants lead their babies that way. Eliza was trying to talk to the elephant without using words, but it wasn't working.

"Go back! It's an electric fence!" Eliza cried to them, but it was no use.

Then she got an idea. She had a necklace in her pocket that her father had given her. She took it out and threw it at the fence. A shower of sparks flew all around it. The elephant stopped, blew a warning cry and turned around. The other elephants followed.

"You did it! You told them to go back!" Eliza cried, hugging the elephant's neck.

Suddenly Bree swooped down in the Blackburn chopper and Sloan grabbed Eliza by the arm. They flew over the churning river and he dangled Eliza over the rapids.

"You will regret this!" he said with rage, dropping her.

"Help!" Eliza gasped as she plummeted into the water. Bree and Sloan turned away in the chopper as the current swept Eliza downstream and dragged her under.

Then, out of nowhere, a hand reached out to save her.

"Shaman Mnyambo!" Eliza gasped. "I'm so sorry I broke the rule!"

"But, Eliza, don't you see?" he said. "You didn't need your gift to save the elephant herd. You saved them with your heart. So I'm granting you back your powers."

"Really? You are?" Eliza said, going to hug him.

Moments later, when an exhausted Eliza walked up from the riverbank, she finally saw her parents.

"Mum! Dad!" she called.

"Poppet!" Nigel cried.

"Ohhh, Eliza!" Marianne said. "Thank heaven you're all right!"

"You're okay and the elephants are saved," Debbie sighed.

"The Shaman even gave me back my powers," Eliza whispered to Debbie after hugging her parents.

"How awesome!" Debbie shouted.

"Shhh!" Eliza said. "It's a secret, remember?"

Debbie looked around. "As I was saying, how awesome that you're okay, Sis," Debbie said loudly, giving Eliza a big hug.

"I'm glad you two are so happy to see each other," Marianne said.

Eliza put her arm around Debbie. "Mum, we actually do worry about each other."

"Yeah," said Debbie and winked. "I guess it's, um, our little secret."